finders keepers

•

Keepers

by WILL and NICOLAS

Voyager Books
Harcourt Brace & Company
San Diego   New York   London

Requests for permission to make copies of any part
of the work should be mailed to the following address:
Copyrights and Permissions Department,
Harcourt Brace & Company, 6277 Sea Harbor Drive,
Orlando, Florida 32887-6777.

Voyager Books *is a registered trademark*
of Harcourt Brace & Company.

Library of Congress Cataloging-in-Publication Data
Will, 1904–1974
Finders Keepers.
"Voyager Books."
Summary: Two dogs each claim a bone they have found
and ask passersby for help deciding ownership.
[1. Dogs—Fiction.]   I. Nicolas, 1911–1973.
II. Title.
PZ7.L6637Fi   1989   [E]   87-8500
ISBN 0-15-227529-0 H616 9602   06/11
ISBN 0-15-630950-5 pb

Manufactured in China

LEO   30 29 28 27 26 25 24 23
4500205779

Two dogs were digging in the yard. One had a spot on his head. His name was Nap. The other had a spot on his tail. His name was Winkle. Scratch, scratch. Scratch, scratch. They never stopped digging for a minute. At last they found a bone.

"That bone is mine," said Nap. "I saw it first."

"It's mine," said Winkle. "I touched it first."

A farmer drove by with a load of hay and his cart bogged in a soft spot on the road.

"Let's ask the farmer," said Nap.

"Suits me," said Winkle. "Whose bone is it, Mr. Haymaker, Nap's or mine? I touched it first."

"But I saw it first," said Nap.

"Just give a hand here at shoving my cart out of the rut and I'll see what I can do," the farmer said.

Nap and Winkle and the farmer and the horse
pushed and pulled and pushed and pulled. And
they hauled the cart out of the rut.

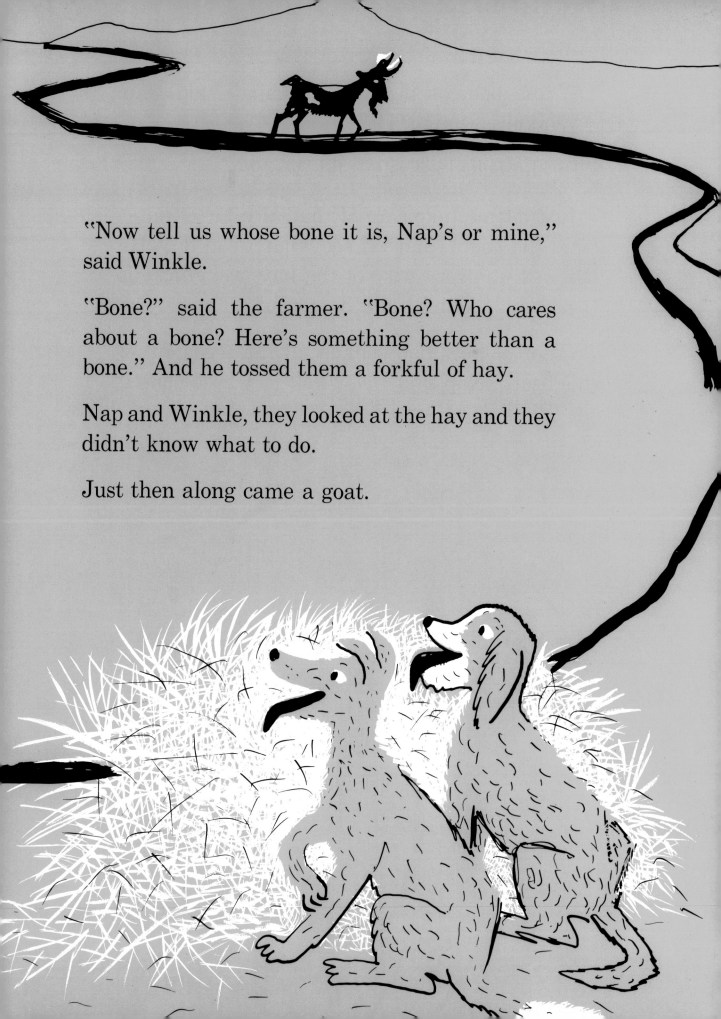

"Now tell us whose bone it is, Nap's or mine," said Winkle.

"Bone?" said the farmer. "Bone? Who cares about a bone? Here's something better than a bone." And he tossed them a forkful of hay.

Nap and Winkle, they looked at the hay and they didn't know what to do.

Just then along came a goat.

"Whose bone is it, Mr. Tuftichin," said Nap, "Winkle's or mine? I saw it first."

"But I touched it first," said Winkle.

"Just let me take care of that nice bit of hay," said the goat, "and I'll see what I can do." He chewed up every wisp of the hay, waggling his beard and looking very thoughtful.

When the goat had shaken all the seeds out of his beard, Nap said, "Now tell us whose bone it is, Winkle's or mine."

"Bone?" said the goat. "Bone? Who cares about a bone? I'll give you some good advice instead. Don't go chasing after a goat unless your teeth are sharper than his horns."

And off he skipped, leaving them no wiser.

Then Nap said, "Let's go down the road a ways and see if we can't find somebody to decide between us."

"Suits me," said Winkle.

They buried the bone and set off down the road. The first person they met was an apprentice barber. He was just learning how to cut hair and couldn't find anybody to practice on.

"Mr. Hairtrimmer," said Nap, "Winkle and I found a bone. Whose should it be, his or mine? I saw it first."

"But I touched it first," said Winkle.

"Just let me trim your hair a bit to try my tools and I'll see what I can do," said the barber.

He went at Winkle's hair with his scissors, clipping and snipping, while Nap looked on and smiled.

Then Nap had his hair cut, while Winkle looked on and smiled.

The barber held his mirror up.

"Suits me," said Winkle, holding himself very straight. Nap laughed.

"Not bad," said Nap, looking very solemn. This time Winkle laughed.

But when they asked about the bone, the barber shrugged his shoulders and said, "Bone? Who cares about a bone? Hair that is neat is better than meat." And he took up his bag of tools and off he went.

Just then a big dog came ambling down the road.

"Nap and I found a bone, Mr. Longshanks," said Winkle. "Whose bone is it, Nap's or mine? I touched it first."

"But I saw it first," said Nap.

"That isn't easy to say," said the big dog, wagging his tail slowly. "What sort of a bone is it?"

"Just an ordinary bone," said Nap.

"Well," said the big dog, wagging his tail a little faster. "You'd better show the bone to me."

Nap and Winkle dug up the bone and the big dog looked at it.

"This is a nice little bone," said the big dog, and his tail went so fast you could hardly see it. "I'll be glad to take care of it for you."

He picked up the bone and
started for the gate. Then
Nap looked at Winkle and
Winkle looked at Nap.

Winkle jumped at the big dog's head, Nap at his tail.

And they bit and they slashed until the big dog dropped the bone and ran off yelping.

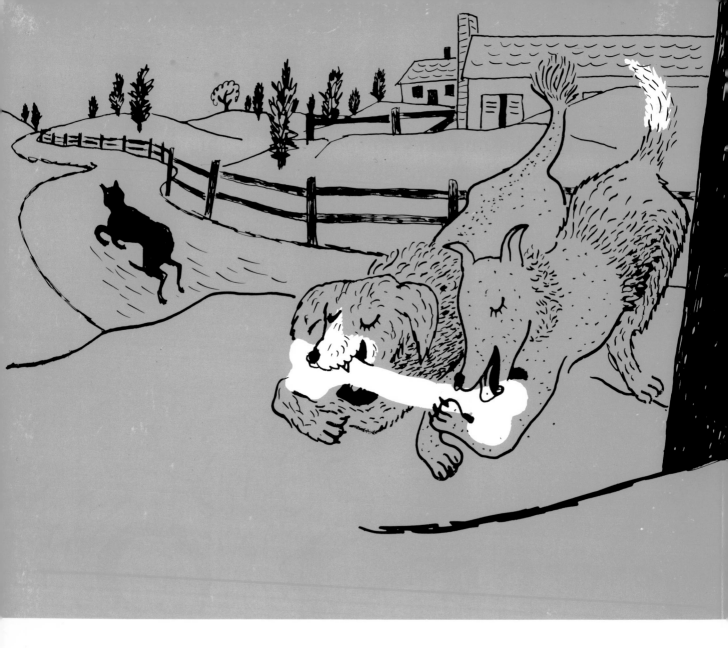

Then Nap looked at Winkle and Winkle looked at Nap. And Nap took one end of the bone and Winkle took the other end of the bone and they both chewed away at it together, without another word.